Young Learner's

Stories from Around the World

The Honest Heir

The Gingerbread Man

Momotaro

Abeni and the Butterfly

The Honest Heir

(A story from China)

The King of China had no children. He held a contest to find his heir. He announced that any boy who wanted to be the future king could come to the palace and receive one royal seed.

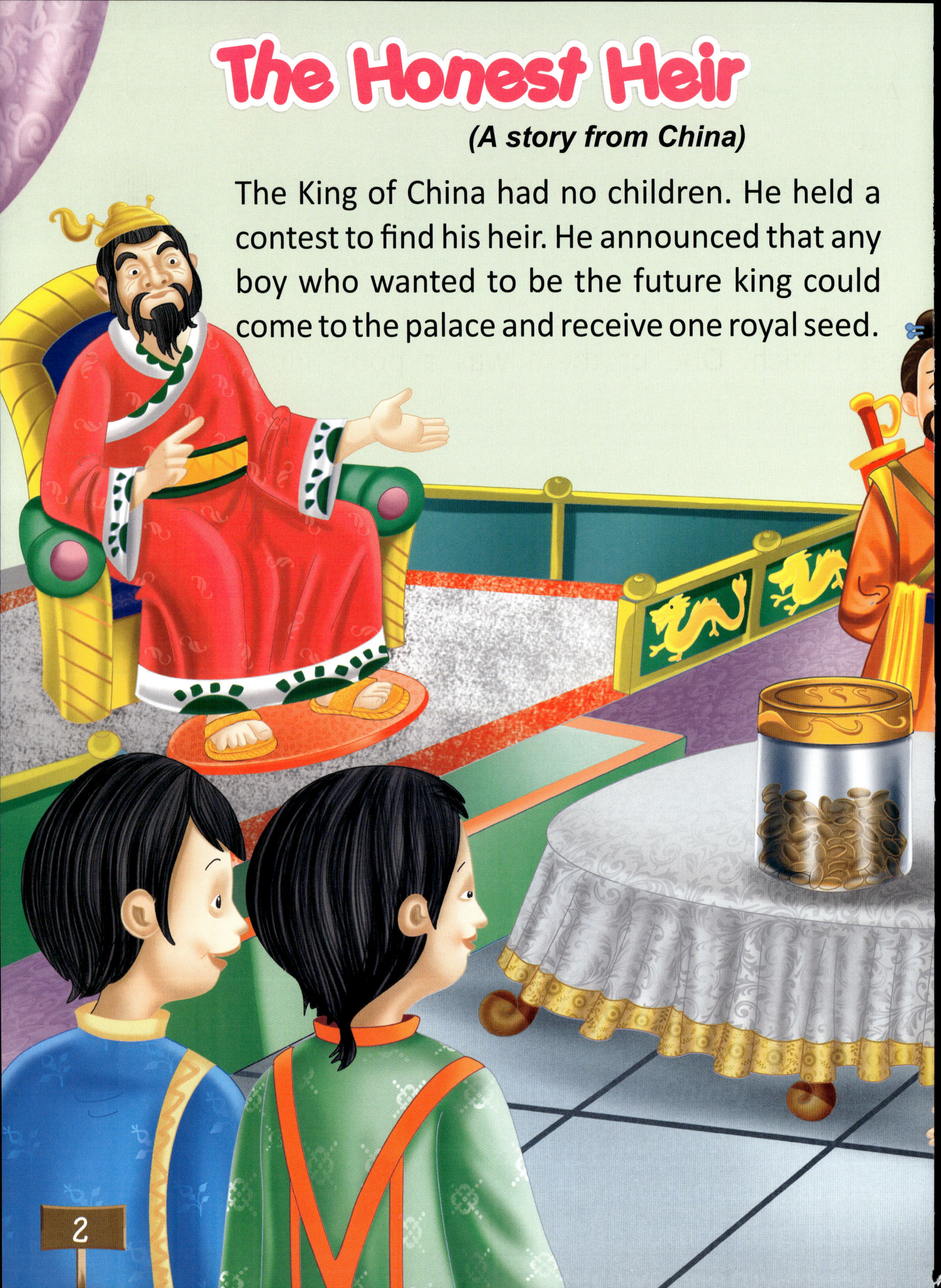

All the boys were to return in two months with their plants. The boy who would succeed in growing the best plant from the seed given to him would become the king. Everyone in the kingdom was excited. Boys from all over China came to the royal palace to collect a seed each. One of them was a poor and honest boy called Jun.

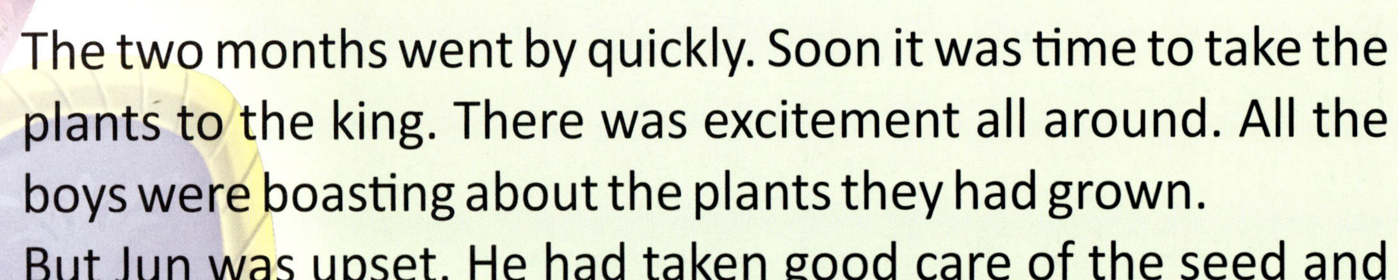

The two months went by quickly. Soon it was time to take the plants to the king. There was excitement all around. All the boys were boasting about the plants they had grown.

But Jun was upset. He had taken good care of the seed and watered it daily, but no plant had grown from the seed. Sad and disappointed, he took the empty pot to the palace. All the boys had brought along beautiful plants. They laughed at Jun's empty pot.

When the king saw Jun's empty pot, he asked, "Where is your plant?"

Jun replied, "Your Majesty, I tried my best but the seed just wouldn't grow."

The king smiled and said, "All the seeds were cooked. They could not have grown into anything. You have been honest. All the others lied to me. I declare you the future king!"

Jun got the reward for his honesty.

The Gingerbread Man

(A story from England)

Once upon a time, there was an old woman. She loved to bake. One day, she baked a gingerbread man. As soon as she let it out of the oven, the gingerbread man came to life!

He hopped out of the plate and ran out of the window. The old woman ran after him.

"Run, run as fast as you can,
You won't catch me,
I'm the gingerbread man," sang the gingerbread man.

He ran out of the cottage and into the farm. A cow tried to catch him, but he sang the same song and ran out of the farm.

The gingerbread man ran out of the farm and into the fields. A scarecrow tried to catch him, but he sang his song and kept running.

Soon, he reached the forest. There he saw a fox and sang his song. But the fox said, “I don’t care. I don’t care. I don’t wish to catch you. I don’t want to eat you.” The gingerbread man stopped running.

"Let's be friends," he said to the fox.

The fox said, "Of course! Come, shake my hand."

As soon as he came close, the fox pounced on him and gobbled him up! The clever fox smiled and sang,

"You can run as fast as you can,
But I'm smarter than you,
Little gingerbread man!"

Momotaro

(A story from Japan)

One day, a woman found a giant peach floating in the river. She took the peach home. When she cut it open, a little boy came out of it. She felt he was sent to her by the Gods! She named him Momotaro. She brought him up well, and he grew up to be a handsome and brave young man.

All was well in their village and everyone lived peacefully. But, one day the demons attacked their village. They looted the houses, killed people and their pets, and destroyed the crops in the fields. Momotaro was very angry. He wanted to take revenge. He got ready to fight the demons. His mother prayed to the Gods and cooked special dumplings for him. He took the dumplings and headed to the demons' village. His pet dog, monkey and pheasant also went along with him.

Momotaro ate the dumplings that his mother had given him. The magical dumplings gave him the strength of fifty strong warriors. Momotaro and his friends entered the demons' den and fought with them bravely. Soon many of the demons were dead and the remaining ran away. Momotaro collected all the riches that the demons had stolen from his village. The entire village celebrated Momotaro's victory over the demons. No one ever attacked the village again, and the people lived happily ever after.

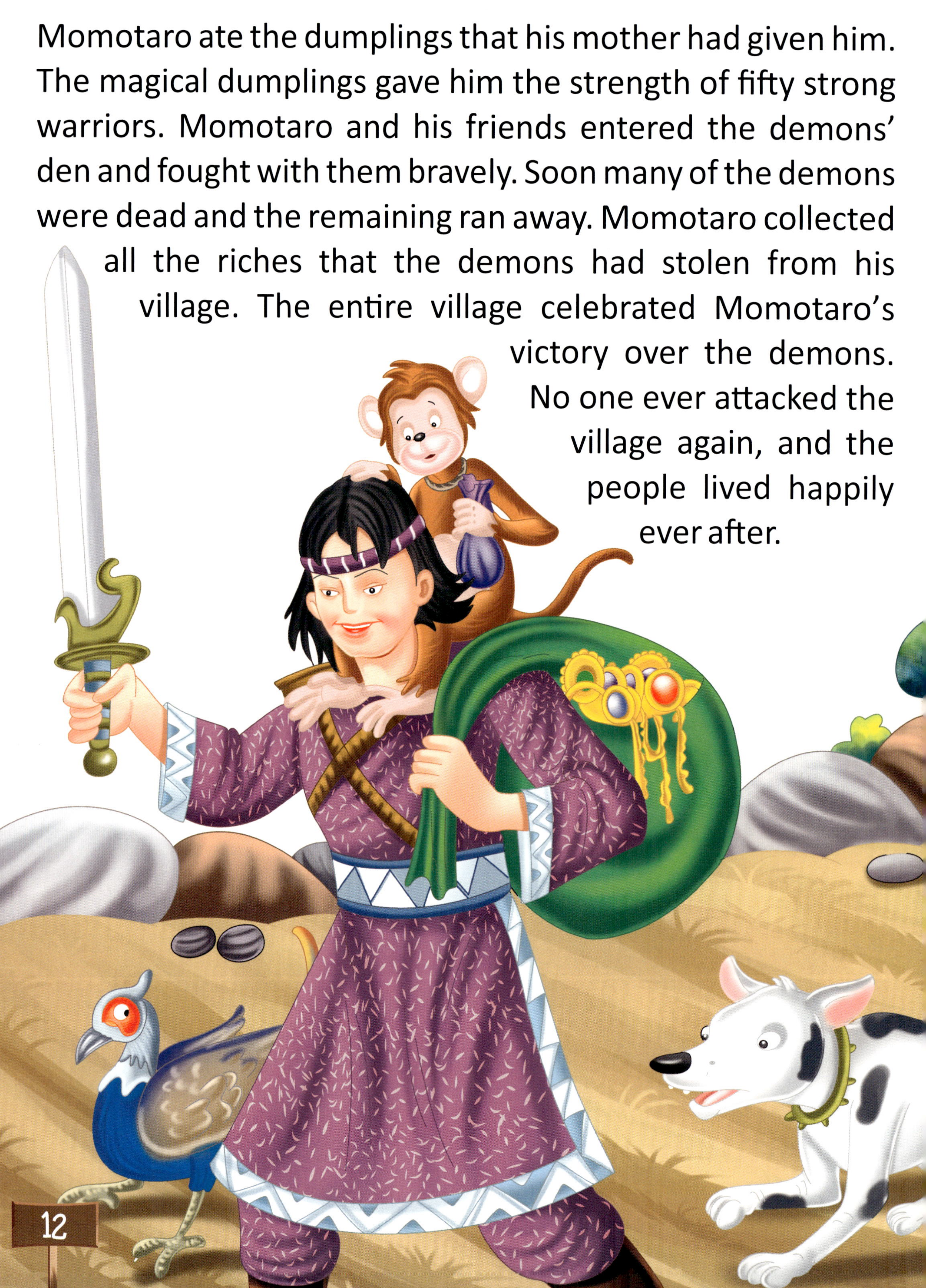

Abeni and the Butterfly

(A story from Poland)

Abeni the ant, was busy gathering food for the winter months. Just then she spotted a tiny tail on a leaf. It seemed to be all wrapped up in something. She did not know that it was a caterpillar.

“Oh! You poor thing. You can hardly move!” Abeni said. “I can run and jump, but all that you can do is wiggle your tail.”

Every day, she passed by the caterpillar, said a few pitiful words and walked away. Then one day, the caterpillar was gone! In its place sat the most beautiful creature Abeni had ever seen. It was a butterfly with bright and colourful wings! Abeni was indeed surprised.

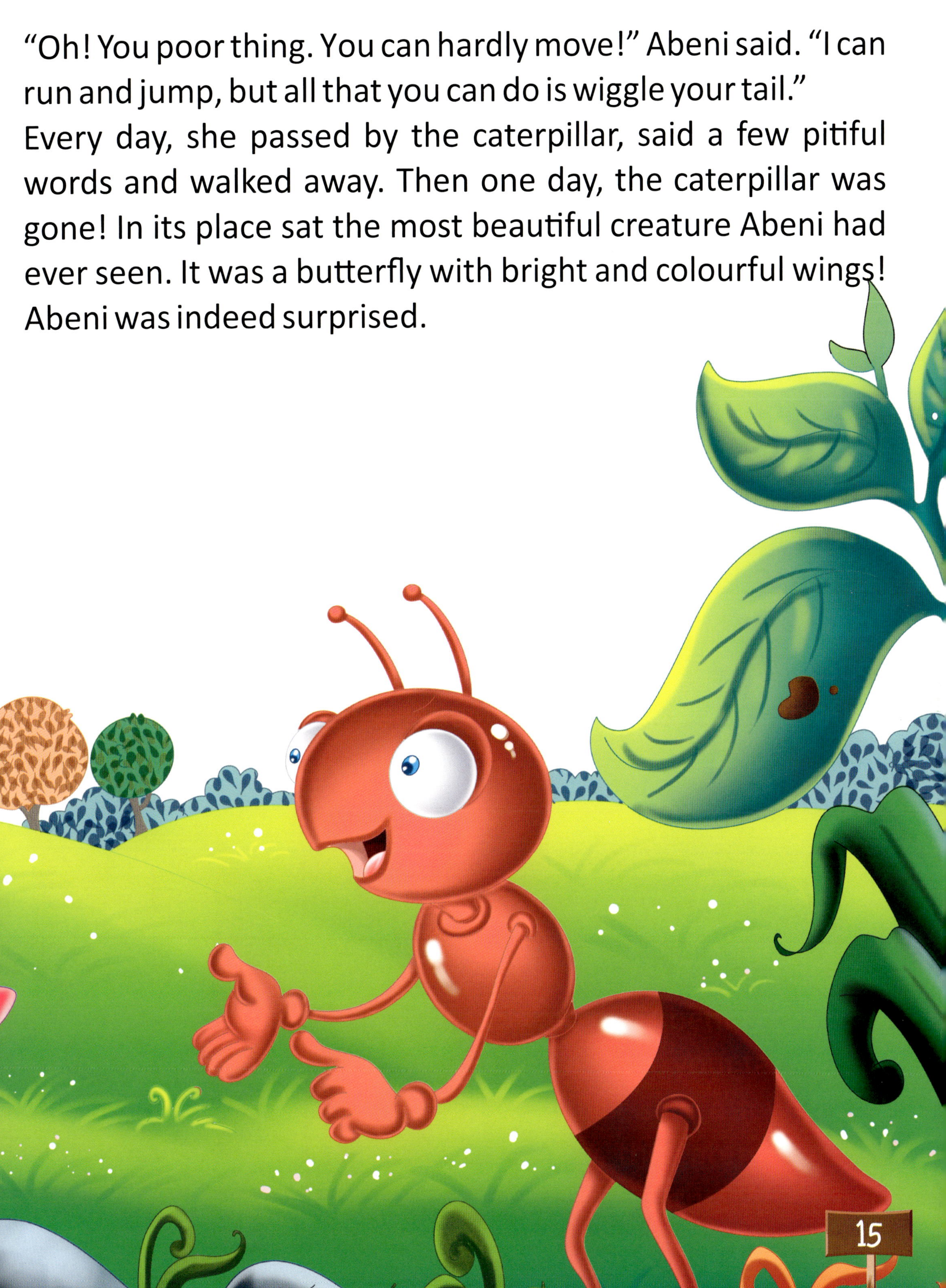

"Don't look so surprised, dear Abeni," said the butterfly. "I am the same caterpillar you felt pity for. You kept saying how you could run and jump and I couldn't. Look at my beautiful wings. I can fly from one flower to another while you can't. But I shall not laugh at you. Each one of us is special in some way. We should never make fun of anyone."

Saying this, the butterfly flew away and Abeni was left standing there, ashamed at her behaviour.